After One

THE HOUGHTON MIFFLIN
NEW POETRY SERIES

Judith Leet, *Pleasure Seeker's Guide*

David St. John, *Hush*

Heather McHugh, *Dangers*

Gerald Stern, *Lucky Life*

Judith Wright, *The Double Tree:
Selected Poems 1942–1976*

Christopher Bursk, *Standing Watch*

Thomas Lux, *Sunday*

James McMichael, *Four Good Things*

Reginald Gibbons, *The Ruined Motel*

Maria Flook, *Reckless Wedding*

Tom Sleigh, *After One*

After
One

Tom Sleigh

HOUGHTON MIFFLIN COMPANY   BOSTON   1983

Library of Congress Cataloging in Publication Data
Sleigh, Tom.
    After one.

    (The Houghton Mifflin new poetry series)
    I. Title.   II. Series.
PS3569.L36A7   1983   811'.54   83-8602
ISBN 0-395-34644-4
ISBN 0-395-34842-0 (pbk.)

Printed in the United States of America

Q 10 9 8 7 6 5 4 3 2 1

For Tamara
and my mother and father

Acknowledgments

I wish to thank the editors of the following magazines for publishing some of the poems that appear in this book: *The New Yorker* — "Three Horses" and "A Formal Occasion"; *The New Republic* — "Jenny Fish"; *The Massachusetts Review* — "Alp"; *Ploughshares* — "In the Hospital for Tests"; *Poetry* — "The Very End"; *Shankpainter* — "The Utter Stranger" and "Uccello."

I also wish to thank The Fine Arts Work Center in Provincetown, Yaddo Corporation, the MacDowell Colony, and the University of New Mexico's D. H. Lawrence Fellowship for aid in the completion of this collection.

My special thanks go to F.B., D.J., C.M., R.P., and B.S. for their support and criticism.

Contents

After One

Logos

You walk on the road accompanied
By dust. Each footprint like a lie
Points to something hidden,
Perhaps something monstrous in the pines.

It cries out, a wail curdling
In the brain. You are too tightly wound
Into yourself to hear,
But again, as if it would tear

The chest from too much grief,
A dark, insistent laugh,
Whether at you or someone else makes
Little difference to the hook

That must be jerking in the throat,
Half-scream now, half-stifled shout
Of warning. You are nearing it,
That epileptic fit

Of light sprawled on a green sheet
Of needles, twisting as if caught
In a gathering net
Hauled upward through the salt

Dark element toward the club,
The pike, that, brilliant with blood,
Speaks its broken
Truth: we are taken, graven

By our birth into the stone
Of the world, a rain-beaten name
Flushed a moment with blood and light.
You are nearing it, nearing it,

Cannot turn or side-step. It pounds
In the dust rising round
Your feet as now it surrounds you
Like the sky going blue

As coal-embers: it speaks you, only you,
Your name's furnace that you pass through.

Words to a Former Musician

for Tim

Your hand that does not reach for mine,
But grips instead a walking-stick
To help you past snow-covered rock,
I recognize at once as mine:
Ten years, twenty, still we're twins.

These mornings that are raw and dark
I ache to hear your slide trombone
Improvise around our hearts
The notes which register the pain
That, growing up, we grow apart

— But your music-years are done;
Left behind with all you were
When practice in a room alone
Made you burn the truest star
Above Hollywood's glaring neon.

You were too gentle to survive,
And flipped one night in Vegas:
Each second gripped you, paralyzed;
The dizzying notes blared to you live
From the golden horns of emptiness,

As in each ear despair contrived
To outplay loneliness . . . Now you're here,
I'm here; and all around us lie
The dead; and past the dead, the river
That, uniformly flowing by,

Marks the boundary line between
What's lost and what's still left to lose:
I'm shocked to see how much we've grown
Beyond our child's-play sticks and stones;
Now words we hurl in anger bruise.

The path we follow skirts the pond
Drowned in snow and hemlocks' gloom,
And only when we crest the rise and find
To our surprise the tower open,
Do we feel the smart of being twins

Who no longer can be brothers.
And yet our boots clomp on the stone,
We climb each step together,
Till at the top the stair narrows and one
Must make way for the other.

And since your fate pushed you first
From where we huddled in the dark
Sharing blood, hunger, and thirst,
I step behind and watch you work
The stone door back, then burst

Dazzled into day that frames
Your stooping silhouette
And wipes away our grown-up shames.
Your smile lights up, lost innocent,
And gives me strength: Stepping forth, it's done.

I join you on the rampart;
And though our eyes refuse to meet,
Between us we hear that shared heart
Whose music's throbbing stop and start
Floods us with a ceaseless beat.

Night Journey

We passed a funeral at midday —
A coffin borne on the shoulders of farmers
In dungarees, the black-shawled, barefooted women
Close behind, and a ragged cortege of waving children —
And at midnight in some plain south of Guadalajara,
We bounced calmly along, unscathed
By a lightning storm. The forking rivers
Of light lit boulders and cactus
Holding out their arms like music-hall conductors,
As rain on the windows beat an impossible tempo,
And flash after flash,
Graven on the air, lit our faces.
Serious and historic, like a General's daguerrotype,
My face hovered in that chaos
Of obsessed ceaseless drumming,
And stared back unconcerned,
Eyes wide with detachment, lips pressed
In a firm line. Courageous? Too foolish
To appreciate the danger? The bus
Passed a fruit truck loaded high with oranges
Gleaming like the cone of a volcano.
Miles and miles and miles, and everything
Rendered strange by hearing it repeated,
The syllables rolling crisply off the tongue.

Toward the setting of the moon
The lurid red of the dashboard
Lit up the hunched driver, the plastic figurine
Of Mary dangling from the rear-view mirror.

The scene, like a tableau, floated detached
From the rest of space,
As if our fate was separate, hinted at
By each jarring sweep of the windshield wipers,
Then erased by mud splashing from a truck.
The driver, in his red twilight, suddenly pumped
The brake, his arms pulling us through the curve
As he looked into the mirror, eyes darting
Up the rows of sleep-numbed faces:
The widow next to me snored, the fat man
With golden rings clutched his wooden birdcages,
His silver buckle rising and falling.
And then the moon, flickering myopically,
Skidded into the wash —
We were plunging headlong
In the night's close tunnel,
The lightning crossing itself
With each jittering raucous flash.

In the morning yawns and coughs broke
In the clear-washed air, as before us, beyond the pines,
The cluster of stucco suburbs
Began to pit the plateau, its slopes
A ruddy chestnut color, eroded and muddy.
The highway broke into four lanes, traffic
A squat black blur of taxis.
Laundry snapping from tenement roofs
Flashed a ragged semaphore.
On the sidewalks the vendors' carts beetled

Back and forth before the subway ramps.
Our driver bowled down the center stripe,
The dangling streetlights flickering wildly,
As block by block traffic slowed
To a thick metallic grinding of gears and sounding horns,
To the tall commercial buildings shadowing the street.
Our baggage hauled from the rack,
We were each the desert traveller mulling over
Home crouched riddling in the heart,
As there and there and there,
Husbands, wives, and sons, all our kin
Suddenly marshalled by a knowing wink or nod,
A finger or hand waved airily through the thickening smog —
O shrouded destination to which we tend,
Will your arms open to receive us?
One by one we pass the driver,
A small lumpy man with warts
Whose molars glint in the lukewarm sun.
Can they hear how our hearts beat,
A faint anticipating drum, as each of us
Slips him a coin and moves to melt into the throng,
An iridescent buoyant mass, surging
Beneath the spray above the hosed-off sidewalk.

Snakes

Lying in sand, I looked for the whale-herd,
The deep-lunged breach misted high
Above the blunt, gleaming, gull-crowned heads.
Sun like a rocket
Smoked in the pines,
As, whittled sharp and clean, hidden in sand,
Two dead baby snakes winked yellow eyes up
Through compass-grass, green bodies just starting
To dry and crack in the dog-day heat.

I prodded them belly up with a cautious foot —
Years back, pail in hand
In the bird refuge swamp, razor-grass nicking my knees,
I bent to the wriggling fury of the nest
And green snakes poured out, shell-shards
Stuck like sequins to their backs,
No mother near, just the cold reptile
Beauty of mating and birth.

I gathered them up, cool and slick like
Re-tread rubber left in a ditch
As they butted the metal lid punched with air-holes,
The sound like rain-drops
Before the cloud-burst. Joy endless and savage
Spread through my chest,
A second sky thin and gaping and pure
Where dizzy I looked down on the bent arrows of flesh
S-curving through roots toward
The reed-bottomed pond

Where the pelican broods in white armadas
Flashed, gliding on the water.

At once, at last, I was the hero
Of my story, pride's gleaming white feather
Blinding my eyes
As opening the lid I watched them weave
Back, green thread into the tapestry of swamp.

And watched the smooth water
As snakes of heat crawled through the air
And felt my heart wet and black
Like clay in a fire
Begin to harden in its wildness, begin to crack,
And leak the knowledge
Of what in the egg we must struggle
To break through to, become, and are.

Jenny Fish

Junior High Prom
Brigham City, Utah

Slender Jenny Fish, you danced with your Dad,
A man dressed darkly with a black bow-tie.
He danced much closer than the rest of us did,
Each step cutting a sharp geometry,

His boxstep divvying the dance floor into squares,
As he held your hand high, the silver sleeve
Tensing like a slot machine lever;
And in your face was no pleasure, just nerve

To keep your pride up, to hide your outrage.
Your dress brushed the tops of your low-heeled shoes
While you followed your Dad as if the edge
Of an abyss widened from the slow-slow

Quick-quick of your pace. We boys gawked amazed,
Unbelieving of the golden chain that yoked
Your glasses to your neck, the flat bodice
Of your dress, so unlike the tissue-padded

Poke of other girls. But how you could dance
Compared to our shambling, how darkly male
Your father looked, as your passion grew dense
And seemed to light your face against the cool

Hard blackness of his suit. None of us dared
For long to watch the turns he would exact,
And, as I remember, I was scared
Before that bleak paternal fact,

Whose every step was a command
Obeyed with furious precision,
As above you, in a fist, your twining hands
Clenched with draconian affection.

La Bufadora

The sea spouts out of rocks and rains down
On the cliffs, drenching the moss
Like water dripping from a beard.
Just so your old vampire pleasure,
The prerogative of mothers,
Goes straight for the jugular, when standing here

You take my arm and point as if I were blind
At the rainbow arching over us,
Strung like faded crepe between the rocks,
At the sun poised like a diver
Behind the tin glitter of the quonset huts.
The cannery workers file along the fence,

Human ants we look down on
From the mountain.
Mother, son, the distinctions come undone
Like the frayed threads of water
Being severed by the wind.
Twenty years in each other's weather,

And still the old tropical refrain
Of storm or shine repeats,
Wearing a groove in our brains
Like a fissure into stone.
Your eyes leap through your horn-rimmed glasses
Like animals through fire,

Taking the scene in fiercely, the weak-lunged son,
The dusted gold of the chaparral.
To you the blowhole is the rumble
Of an Aztec god, perverse in its persistence
At wearing a tunnel through the rock.
Gnarled and bent like the bushes, your voice

Shouts, "Look son! would you look at that!"
Both of us looking down, the dented enamel
Of the ocean pounds the jetty . . .
When you bend your head to hear my watch,
I hear the tick of moonlit stones dragged
In the tide's maternal suck.

The Very End

for my Grandmother

My eyes are strange to the print tonight;
Nero, Caligula, their crimes disappear.
Instead, a pair of button-shoes you wore,
False teeth, a veil, a monogrammed bracelet,
Blot the Roman sun with their antiquity;
And risen in its place, you dust or cook,
Read the latest in child psychology,
Your gloved voice threatening, "Wouldn't you like ... "
Yes, it is miraculous to think of you
At all, what with history droning names
Pricked by the triumvirate, Oblivion,
Epitaph, Farewell. Even to see you
Surface above your facts, the dates marked for birth,
Marriage, death, asks that I float you on my breath.

Three Horses

Out in the pasture, in the clear twilight,
They move through the breast-high alfalfa.
Their broad backs gleam. The mare canters, then trots,
Her two daughters close behind. She slows, paws

The dust that rises to her fetlock,
While the others stretch their legs to a gallop,
Their paths veering off, as all three, separate,
Walk in the velvet softness of their shadows.

Their tails brush away the winged voices
In the dark, their ears twitch, their nostrils flare
And wrinkle. The soft muzzles lower to graze.
The silhouetted curves of their necks disappear,

Then arc up above the green. Like a wave
That carries to shore some slight common thing,
Darkness streams across the desert. Unobtrusive
In this quiet, unaware that what they bring

Into the freshness of the meadow air
Is a grace that lasts beyond the glow
Now melting off the peaks, they step over
The dry ditch into a waterfall of shadow

And turn to face the distance, the stars struck
Like sparks by the far-off clop of thunder,
To the lightning's shattered alphabet
Scribbling on the dusty slate of the air

A message they alone can decipher.
The mare tosses her mane. With bowed head she
Snuffs the criss-cross of her and her daughters'
Track, her blind muzzle deep in the joy

Of their mingled scent. Nickering through the night,
She sidles off toward the lower pasture,
Hooves scraping, neck bowing in the moonlight.
Her daughters prick their ears, but do not answer.

History Lesson

Hamstrung, your genitals hang down, the hair
Has lost its wire.
Someone titters in the rear of the class
But your eyes, unaware they will focus
In bleary celluloid's untime,
Stare us soft and darkly hollow.
Our eyes, rooted between your pelvic bones,
Are shocked that your body's molded flow

Is less than human: Your bones stick out like spines
Against the skin,
As if your skeleton fought to rip loose
From the sagging flesh's current, drag it safe
To our feet, children darkly
Knowing that something monstrous
In your unreeling world has been unleashed.
Dread bleats from your blackened, jittering eyes

As the guards, grainy in their uniforms,
Prod you into line.
Your gaze, jumpy, sweeps the aisles, its appeal
As habitual as the rain that falls
Like needles from the frozen
Heavens. Fingers splayed, stiffened
By cold, from the tattooed wrist your hand hangs
Lynched. The sexless, genderless human

File locks in a frieze that jams in our brains
Even as the film
Jerks it toward the lintel. Sprockets pluck your strings,
Your gaze drags numbly imploring
To us, good, scared, studious children.
One second more, twenty-four
Halt frames, and you hurtle through the door
To the fosse's slush, an unknown, not quite human

Flicker sprayed across the milky screen.
Leader claps on
The spooling rim, as blackness, spilling
On the mind's blank film, blossoms again
To anonymous man tramping
Machine-like to extinction.
But your eyes blaze like twin projector beams
Until the rinsing, neon cloud drifts down.

Judas Waking

His name, his habits, burnt off like a foul gas,
Had left him all the warmth of bedclothes
And blankets, had left his eye untrammeled,
So as he looked, he felt the impartial

Nature of the room, the rocker, the hassock
With kapok poking out, the placid clock's
Glowing numbers. And outside too, darkness
Skating up the ice-glazed hill to the press

And melt of stars, he saw no harshness
In the glitter weighing down the pines, no kiss
Of betrayal hunting the moon's cheek, swollen
To such ripeness in the light-scrubbed pane

That the gleam rousing in the stubble of the field
(Earthlight wound on the star-spoked wheel)
Rose like a prayer to that cleansing fever.
This, if anything, seemed the green pasture

Where never again would he have to want.
But when he shut his eyes, his heart's clear jet
Surging up to scour the dark, his name's
Pestilential star plunged through the crumbling

Roof of night. And then he heard far off
The shrill of gulls converging on a life
He'd never meant. Pierced by the fulgence
Rising from the earth, to the sweating glass

He pressed his lips and stared — in his ears
His heartbeat swamped like surf above the clamor
Swooping on the rocks. No wife, no child,
No one with whom to talk, feverish, scared,

The reflected eyes gave back the pain, the moon's
Exhaustion in the worn air, its ghost-fleshed passion
Spent. Naked, shivering, he hugged himself,
But no heat took the chill from that embrace.

The Utter Stranger

homage to Allen Tate

                    Late summer, clear sky,
Mountains scarred by July fires, fruit trees
Picked bare, Brigham Young's blessed valley

Seen in the unstyed brightness of a boy's
Deathless eye: Green combustion of the lawns
Lay drowned in sprinkler-spray lifting the rainbow's

Manic gleam like a scythe above the town.
Light drained from off the boulders, the glow
Seeping to where I stood on my way down

From the mountains, the rock-ribbed shadows
Darkening the cradle of the valley as they
Hunched shoulder to shoulder, the broken brow

Of the sun pouring flame on the antennae
Nailed like crosses to the sky, goldenrod
Streaming into the wind's translucent eye.

Then clicking of the baseball card
Against the whirring spokes, the headlong
Coast downhill and snap of the cord

Of gravity, then the swift glide, strong
Fluid stroke of the pedals' downward pump,
Heart beating its inward song

To the flesh, streets propelled into the hump
Of the maddened sun, until the corner
And driveway, darkness lying slumped

Beneath the shrubs. Around the corner
Of the house into the belly of the shade
And there, before me, the utter stranger:

Head pitched forward, knees bent as if to wade,
Feet heavy like the hands, body plumb
To the wall, skin tinged the blue shade

Of death beneath the tan. I stood there, numb,
Touched the cropped black hair. I asked
The name, heard the forehead thud. Thumbs

Curled in the palms. The body swayed. Frayed
Strands of rope around the neck chafed the skin.
He swung inside my head, flesh gravid

Under mine, the weight like an anchor pulling
Me through dark water, the enormous hush
Of evening drifting down and down.

At last they cut him loose, laid him in the grass.
Twilight bruised his face as the neighbor man's
Breath exploded in his lungs: But the eyes

Stared sightless through the deeps of the elm.
His air, his space, his light were equally claimed
By all, spoils that fall to life. And though his jaw hung

Slack, it was no tooth of sanction
Or acceptance of what the living
Are careful to call grace that gleamed

From the dark privacy of that mouth.

Uccello

"Ah Paolo, this perspective of yours
makes you neglect what we know for what
we don't know. These things are no use ..."
                                         DONATELLO

The world holds out its threat and hope: he looks
To where the lines, targeted to vanish,
Meet in the bright eye of a bird. The chalk,
Euclid, he forgets. His wish

Becomes the world, a miracle: a bird that weeps,
Not from any sadness, but to bring
It closer to the human. That night, asleep,
He sees the white wings open:

Where feathers were, is now flesh — the beak, flesh,
The torso, human, and now the wings, spread,
Slicked with gold, moult, drop their feathers. The lashes
Flick open, the eyes weep;

A tear falls, perfectly foreshortened;
The eyes stare, washed clean. The throat-feathers
Pulse, whistle. He thinks, *It is not human.*
He reaches out, fingers

Searching for the Form: he draws the figure,
The white feathers at its feet, each tip
Overlapping as they spiral out like stars
Across the paper's void,

Filling it with a brilliance that he must squint
To see against, the human shape he has sketched
Hard at its center, the perspective bent
Back to where it touches

The painter who puts down his tools, thinks:
The angel weeps. Why does he weep? Alive, whole,
The tears fall. In each globe like an ark
He sees his face, full —

The anguished words unknot in his throat:
"I am Paolo of the Birds, Paolo Uccello."

Musicke of Division

Spring is dead. The leaves' fat mature laughter
Repeats our own, halts, grows hysterical
Again. The wind lifts neat and surgical
From the grass, the hoof-gouged field moults its scars,
New moon, new moon, new moon . . . Stars grime the black.
Geese or leaves, something stirs in the air.
Our voices are a wall we climb to hear
Our bodies' aging backtalk: your side aches,
Causes unknown, my urine's streaked with blood.
The room is a shower of newspapers,
Atrocity flattened into words. Our
Furor to change in the seasons' stead
Registers like guns pointed to our heads,
The chambers clicking off like drops of blood.

In the Hospital for Tests

A dripping, numbing girl, surf tearing her
In half, stands in monstrous silhouette
Before a phallus of plate-glass
Smeared with the sun's endless honey.
This is the kind of place where dying could be easy,
The dazzle of the ocean like the flashbulbs of paparazzi.

Or else you lose yourself in this wilderness of dots:
Sun grazing backs of elephants, gazelles,
And there, the ubiquitous girl, teeth awesome
As a lion, arm stretched forth in bronzed
Suspension toward the scorched volcano's head
Bandaged in ice and snow . . . To put off our mortal dress

And inhabit that deathless flesh, air-brushed to divinity —
In a room where we can't see, a pant, gasp, scream
Invades these ad-man's views of Eden. Our eyes jerk up
From the tattered magazines, meet and slither off,
As, dragged up from the bowels, a grunt and bludgeoned groan
Advertise to what extremes —: far gone into beasthood

The vocal chords' crystal cracks, shattering in the throat;
The sun's lion-eye glares from the linoleum,
As we shift and fidget in our chairs, or sit rigid
As if straps of steel bound our hands and feet.
Foreheads crowned with sweat, like the throwing of a switch,
We hear that electrifying pulse scorching in the corridors,

Its naked hurt pouring such contagion in our ears
That we know this cry is mortal: To lift this heaviness,
This dreadful, thorn-pierced paw stretched
Helplessly toward me, the feral, glassy eyes imploring
Numbly for my touch — but I know, we know
How this, how we will end. In this rickety temple,

This braying bag of blood and bone, I hear my heart's
Astonished beat and know no prayer or curse
Sufficient unto that sound. And now the scream fades away,
Though its echo, like the smell of Lysol, still surrounds us.
From the golden broil and char of another sunset ocean
A shatteringly simple girl with my face, my hair,

Stares from a jungle atoll lost deep inside my brain.
The waves, arching their backs, lay down flat at her command,
Purring adoration, licking her golden feet.
In her blindfold of dark glasses, I see the sun's intestines
Ripping into flame as on her lips a smile of wide-eyed
And lacerating gaiety darkens to a firm, untroubled line.

The Invalid

He rose late most mornings and took a walk
Just after the fog had cleared, so the damp
Was still thick in the air, though you could almost
Feel it being sucked into the sun. Spring
Was like that — rain, heat, rain, then a green so sharp
It seemed to hurt your eyes.
                                    I went along,
But only now and then; he preferred to go
Alone. He had a special place just past
The church, an abandoned garden which grew
A ragged ear of corn and some cabbages
That lasted far into the winter;

The snow would tuck like a collar into
The bottom leaves so that they looked like
Blind men wrapped in mufflers to the eyes.

But it was spring that really drew him,
Just before the leaves clustered too tight
To see the bay, and across the bay, the sudden
Glint of the rails.
                            The mist always hung there
Longer, and often you could see it pierced through
By the glimmer shooting off the steel. He'd worn
Down a corridor through the weeds and brambles,
And below, in a half-circle, was a grove
Of dogwood, the blossoms melting through the mist,
Or else the mist condensing into blossoms.
At the edge of the slope he'd kneel and smoke,

While I'd see what was coming up through the weeds
In the garden. He never seemed to take
Much interest in talking then —
                              so we
Would listen to the whine of the train wheels,
Which seemed to echo up a scale pitched higher
Than human ears. It was so clean and pure
That you thought metal rubbing metal
Was the truest tone of grief, as if the loss
Had been so sharp that nothing else could be
Remembered, nothing else felt except
The quaver of the tone as it ascended
Through the mist toward the sun. He heard it
With a love I could never understand,
Though who knows what he heard, he never said
A word about it. The sound made me sad,
And then a little angry, it seemed
Too insistent, too ready to be heard —
But he loved it, it was plain from his face
And the sudden calm in his hands, they shook
Even then, ever so little, and if you watched
Them long, you wondered if they'd been witness to some
Early touch that had frightened them forever.

The shrillness mounted as if the rails grudged
The wheels their ability to move,
Like they wanted to halt some awful
Momentum. Perhaps the groove was too wide,
Or the track too narrow, or the brake

Was simply thrown and all that screeching
Was just routine. It lasted only
A few minutes and then he'd be ready
To amble home, though we always stopped to touch
The burns at the tips of a dogwood bloom.

Refuge

I

A premonition in the marsh
Rose up with all the gangly strength
Of a heron taking flight.
Your black eyes watched the harsh sunlight

Doubling upwards through the reeds.
Joy worked its twist into your smile,
As silence, balanced on one leg,
Stood minted on the sun.

Our shadows reached across the road,
Heads and shoulders in the ditch,
Your hand uplifted to your brow.
I watched your shadow laugh your laugh

As our shadows crossed and uncrossed.
The smoky cavity of dusk
Gorged on our silhouettes.
We couldn't tell which was which.

II

A cage of shade entraps the bed
— Stripes of shadow from the window bars.
The news that you are dead has come
As small surprise, from the tousled head

Now sleeping. The pillows mount like stone
Behind her, her sighs still foreign
As the shouting newsboys
Hawking *El Diario* in the street.

The brass bedposts are bright as tears
That will not fall. Remembrance
Grafts itself to grief, as your face,
Swaying in the bloodshot air,

Rejects its place in heaven's choir
For us, here, this nowhere.
And so I watch you, and watch you weep,
And watch the wings in the scything reds

Of the smog-flawed sun, beat upwards.

Obsequies

for my Grandfather

We stood in line like the deeper vowels
In an alphabet of grief, each sounding
Last inarticulate respects to the lead-cloaked
Thing sent straight from the hospital,

A forgotten prop for the embarrassing
Dumb show. The black trousers,
Neatly hemmed about the stump the doctors
Claimed was your only chance, wrung

Out of you any trace of the human.
Your one black shoe, gleaming, sharp-toed,
Was a dancer's ready to explode
Into motion, tapping out on the coffin

The Morse code rendition of Rest-in-Peace.
My uncle's soft-shouldered wife blew smoke
In your face when she bent to kiss the mis-sloped
Cant of your brow that the autopsist

Had sawed in half to certify your tumor.
Your body bloated to swell the suit,
Threatening at any moment to levitate
To heaven, leaving the necktied farmers

Strangling in three-piece polyester
Free to roll up their sleeves and swill the punch.
Last in line, I could still hear the munch
Of your jaws as you ripped chaw after chaw

From the plug of Beechnut tobacco, then spat
In the Folger's can, one stationed in the cab
Of each truck and tractor, by your bed
And the reclining rocker where your head

As you nodded sank to your deep-furred chest.
Dreaming, you mumbled advice to the President,
Exhorting, "We've a long row to hoe." Bent
Before you, my gaze snipped the threads, thumbed the lids

Back: your eyes were the straight still blue of diesel
Smoke, when, with the grease-gun cocked in hand,
You gazed into the blare of the dust-hazed sun,
Then rammed the barrel to the iron nipple.

The Necessary Webs

Night falls over and over,
    Earth turning on its axis
        As the trees fulfill the dusk ...

The chair, the kettle on to boil,
    The radio antenna bathed in a thousand
        Choiring voices, foreshadow the calm

That settles like fine ash
    In this room where, surrounded
        By my life, I glow, the only thing

Alive. They blur into the backdrop
    Of my death, when years from now,
        Or tomorrow, or the moment after now,

I start upward from my body
    Through the sky of constellated
        Beings that have kept me

Ruthlessly in life, as I have tangled
    Them in my necessary webs, spinning
        From my guts the gentle thread

To bind them closer, as once with you, Father,
    Clinging to the edge of sleep
        In the narrow dark of a motel bed,

We talked about our deaths,
        The moment when each of us
            Breathes the soul's smoking tinder

Into the lungs of the unborn.
        Eyes shut, talking on and on
            In the intimate sadness of speech

A man reserves for his son
        When he himself has lost a father,
            You curled your hand into mine,

Your knuckles' bony protest sharp
        Against my palm, as if to resist
            The blood-web ravelling between us,

Where wrapped in love of each other
        For the shared terror of our flesh,
            We dangled, suspended on a flying

Thread of sleep like a spider that re-weaves
        The ragged center of our lives
            Until the savage feathered clock begins to sing.

Land's End Dialectic

Januaries the tall sea
Attacks the tilting lighthouse.
Will we ever be free of these foaming sallies
On the mutability of sand?

The pounding waves leave a chalky residue
Frozen in billowing ruffles like lace mantillas.
Even a walker's footprints gain solidity
As they run at and past him, in a hurry

To get where he just came from, the fingernail
Of the long pitted finger crooked suggestively
Toward the mainland. Washing, always washing!
Who could stand such cleanliness in the daily routine

Of getting comfortable with the dirt
The world offers? Or is this
Grating assault of element on element
The sea's last word on honesty?

But the lighthouse spinning dizzily
Hasn't time for nice distinctions, confronting
Such towering feats of strength
As wind and water in a freezing lather

Work up in a moment's hilarity:
Clouds blue-black torn from the stiff horizon
Pummel the iron helmet of the light
With rain, its sheet-glassed, white-faced,

Lead-paned brow undaunted somehow
In its piercing stare. Does it see truly to the heart
Of the blackening squall, the waves that pile
Like paper selves, each giving up the ghost

To the one behind in a rising wash of foam?
Here safe at home one can watch and think
Dry thoughts — though a lowering cast on the mind's brink
Hints at the smoke in last night's dream.

Alp

The mountain, harsh, redolent, green,
Lets down its shadow.
I walk unseen on the upper slopes,
The peaks bivouacked above me.
The urgent stream rushes from stone bowl to stone bowl,
Frothing with its message of cold.

Pistol shots crack beneath the glacier.
The sun holds out a hand to the crippled river
Limping round conspiracies of boulders.
How simple the life of the deserter,
High and irresponsible among the eternal, elemental . . .
Frozen moments of moss and lichen,

Yellow and red beards that do not wag
Or wrangle with Teutonic incomprehension,
Here I am home, my mind unlaced
Like a garment of last century.
Each breath strikes steel into my lungs.
The sky wobbles on the peak of each dizzy, floating alp.

Endless air opens its mouth at my feet.
The unbottled perfume of the valleys ascends,
Clash of roosters, trumpets, the hallucinating drums.
At my back the peaks wall up, Hannibal's elephants,
The crush of history swaying forward,
Crunching in my footsteps to the rim.

The Painter

I knew a painter once, though not exactly
A painter — an embryo, let's say, a man
Who feels himself in paint, but rarely gets
The feeling right.
               We were neighbors for a time
When each of us was doing nothing, though
I was steadier at it than he was,
And he admired my dedication. I guess
He felt we had no future, and thinking back
To who we were, I'd have to say he's right —
For himself, I mean, I've done some things
That in the telling come off well, though later
I wonder why I bothered. Perhaps
He scared me with that clear eye that knew
The broadly imagined future had
A way of shrinking to the narrowest
Of corridors.
             Yet he used the sky
The way an ostrich uses sand, content
To recount his dreams or practice magic
With an antique sword . . .
                He'd read Crowley
And the rest, admired everything in Yeats
I couldn't stand, talked of the unconscious
Like "a high grove of trees in a sudden wind."
His painting was like that, though I thought
Of something crouching, out of fear or sheer
Defiance. He painted my portrait once,
Took the feeling from my eyes and put it

In my hands about to clench the bone handle
Of a knife. There was no knife in the picture,
Just my face and hand upraised toward the viewer,
My elbow cropped out. It looked in the background
Like the stifling of an explosion,
Though all that force seemed like a pressure
That kept the figure from flying apart.

I was impressed he'd seen so clearly what
I'd hidden or tried to doubt —
                              to see yourself
Like that, so sublimely ugly, you wondered
How others missed it — well, perhaps they don't,
But I've tried to dress a bit more neatly,
Though the effect seems often just grotesque
(You lose your faith in compliments that way).

"Art is something you do today, for today,"
He said, having listened, as he painted,
While I read *The Golden Ass* aloud.

A Formal Occasion

The tidal flats stretched far and awkward,
Leaving the battered, barnacle-covered
Pilings of the pier naked, knee-deep in mud.
Music from a restaurant ebbed away from us,
Then rushed to where we stood, growing louder,
More substantial, like a champagne glass
Filling up. A wedding party, a reunion,
Something family — but nothing to do with us.

The lighthouse, the sky unravelling into reds,
The mussel-picked jetty rocks — it was a shock
How all of it interlocked,
Then broke apart for no reason we could say.
Where the clammers had spaded and trowelled
Declared itself distinct
From the golden wash of marsh grass,
And the gulls' blank cries, tugged behind
The fishing boat like unsold balloons,
Made a landscape — skyscape, rather — of their own.

The boat veered toward the fingernail
Of sand as if to beach, but abruptly
Righted and chugged toward the pier.
The nets dripped and shone. A sudden rose-flush
Through the clouds dyed the flats deep
Purple and the beacon lit up, an emerald
Finger stroking the arching wake,
An arrow of foam.

We picked our way back
As the tide, coming in, began to
Surround the reedy hummocks. Shellfish
Squirted jets of water at us,
A miniature water garden. This time
We walked right by the party —
Tuxedos, ties, women dressed in chiffon,
All of them comfortably, distantly talking
Behind the broad clean window. A woman
Smiled at us, a man in a silk vest
Turned his back, also smiling.

By this time we had to hurry, the flats
Were receding beneath the tide — ribbons
Of water crisscrossing through
The jetty knotted into a river,
The lighthouse light thickened to an arm
Energetically parrying with the shadows.

We stopped, utterly taken by the sweep,
Not romantically taken, not seeing it as us
Or in any way like us, but as we'd seen the party,
From a distance, behind glass, glad to be
Only looking in, free to pass. The town,
Windows flushing, was quiet, a perfect
Quiet, somehow warm and vacant,
Like a bird that is asleep. The cold
Glazed our faces, a cold we didn't mind;

The music blurred, dwindled, disappeared,
Utterly unasked for, yet wholly given,
A gift utterly used up. Already the flats
Were warping in moonlight. We turned
Our backs to the view, we walked along.

Lullaby

Bellying out in the full sail of dream,
I lie like a flame going down in the trees,
The pine whisper in air blossoming like desire

By the upper creekbed where bumblebees
Lay stunned in the black-eyed Susans.
Flesh of the world opens to flesh of the air,

As light gathers and pools in the boughs
And drifts nervously down across rock and dirt.
My hands find your hair in the bedroom dark

Of mid-afternoon, and I see the pale mark
My fingers leave on your cheek. The dark's
Softness ushers me deeper into the trees,

Into the slopes' upriding green. The sky
Crests into sky where a blue feather drops,
Tumbles, is lost in the needles. Your hips curve

In a motion that questions the dark, the quiet,
The blind touch flesh tells us is the heart's
Truth and longing. Sunlight slants through

The curtain, the pale beam's soft yoke
Falling on our shoulders, the music echoing
And drifting in the breath between notes.

After One

Pen marks trying to scratch their way to sense
As, here beneath the lamplight, the present
Refuses to let me parse Experience,
Saying, "What for? A cigarette, a dent
In a fender, a knife at the throat,
The old young men careering in the street,

She's gone, you're an audience of one,
So what for?" Language, unbidden at the door,
Knocks like moonlight to be allowed to enter —
It's as if a body remembered in sun
Returned in darkness to squander that saved light:
Your legs, long and strenuous, your calves, flexed tight,

Pedal your bicycle around and around
The vacant stadium of the mind
Where I, the sole spectator, cut off from you
By this cloud of exhaled smoke, by chance
And distance that weaves by day and unweaves
By night, must squint to seize that blur who

Raced along my nerves before she was pulled
Beyond my orbit — though unaccountably stalled
In this bedroom's rented dark, a ghost
Who walks each creaking board, each telltale crack,
Who moans in the aching, overheated radiator.
How hard it is to forget to remember

Your palm pressed to the teacup's curving breast,
As you sip and sip, steeped in your heart's quiet.
Steam mists your brow thrust forward into light
That, like a wave, sprays across your cheek
To the gleaming faces of the fresh-rinsed plates
Mirroring one another in the rack . . .

But features crack, flake off like rain-soaked plaster,
The blessed enclosures built on thigh and lip
Bulldozed overnight to a plain's clean sweep . . .
Losing (I believe it) is no disaster,
But for once I wish my recompense
Was not this blistering isolation that hisses

Like a secret to the ear in the chest,
Condemning my hand to this inkstained idleness
In which someday your eyes may change color,
Your hair retain its labored curl forever
(Rollers and bobby-pins all hurled into the dust),
Or your face, ironclad in loveliness, need no touch

Of make-up, revised (embalmed?) in my own image.
Two pairs of eyes thrust into each other,
And then, almost as quickly, drift out of sight.
So I wish I could smoke an ultimate cigarette,
One that would burn from youth to old age,
And at the final puff, gently scatter

The accumulated ash of all that happened;
And reveal to me those nights that shone
With nakedness and naked talk, with gentleness
Palpable as a hand clutched in sleep . . .
Outside in the street tears of broken glass
Shimmer on the face of the asphalt deep.

It's after one, and as I write you down,
You pedal further and further, now a streak
Receding down endless lengths of roadway
That narrow to a point of dark that locks
My eye in dimness, and you are gone.
But in my hand I hold a turning key

That even as I lay it down goes on turning.

To the Other

You leave, gray as the mist, the way a shadow
Leaves the house, and in your hands are your cornet,
Your paper sack, and before you the snowbound walk,
The long silent one to school past the statue in the park
And the sagging net in the tennis court —
The net ripped and useless, the arc lights long since burned out —
Past the grove of evergreens
Where you breathed rank needles and damp earth;
Past the willow limbs, long-boned,
Fountaining to the ground, scratching in the snow
A nervous, wind-tossed scrawl;
To the pond where your toy motorboat
Floated adrift in the autumn sun,
Its light lazing off the water
Onto the undersides of leaves, gray-green
In the spangled calm lapping slower
And slower to this abandonment
And hush, to the chill, concentrated
Darkness that locks the surface in first ice —
And there, as if by miracle, dredged up from the muck,
Shines the frozen fire of leaves ...

And now you step forth, the utter Stranger,
From behind the dream's disfiguring mask, —
The ageless eyes that seize the future
Insistent with the knowledge
Life bends down to impart —:
And when you let me look,
All the light I wrenched from darkness — a light

That whispers like a night-light to a sleeping child,
That seals his heart into its warmth, its mildness, —
Its mildness of a child who whispers
To the night that whispers to the child
That he is dreaming, that there is nothing
In the closet but the headless overcoats,
The black umbrellas shrivelled to headless stalks,
That there is nothing, nothing —

                          until he wakes
And the light is there, he is there, the light
That whispers that the world will never die . . .
The world that in your eyes' transforming radiance
Is a folded paper crown withering into sparks —
The light floats and flickers far away,
Ignorant, meaningless . . .

                  Your face shines down
On the shuddering ice, the cold reluctant
Flesh drawn white and taut as string
Around the knuckles of the branches and warped
A thousand glittering ways across the night.